JOKE BOOK

No part of this work may be reproduced in whole or in part, or stored in a retrieval system, or transmitted in any form or by any means, electronic, mechanical, photocopying, recording, or otherwise, without written permission of the publisher. For information regarding permission, write to Scholastic Inc., Attention: Permissions Department, 557 Broadway, New York, NY 10012.

ISBN: 0-439-64162-4

DreamWorks' Shark Tale TM & © 2004 DreamWorks L.L.C.
Published by Scholastic Inc.

SCHOLASTIC and associated logos are trademarks
and/or registered trademarks of Scholastic Inc.

12 11 10 9 8 7 6 5 4 3 2 1   4 5 6 7 8 9/0

Designed by Kay Petronio
Illustrations by Ken Edwards

Printed in the U.S.A.
First printing, September 2004

DreamWorks
Shark Tale ™

JOKE BOOK

Jesse Leon
McCANN

SCHOLASTIC INC.

New York   Toronto   London   Auckland   Sydney
Mexico City   New Delhi   Hong Kong   Buenos Aires

Oscar

Living on squid row, he dreams of becoming a superstar fish

Lenny

A vegetarian shark, and that's the meat of the problem

Angie

An angel of a fish who has fallen for Oscar — hook, line and sinker!

Lola

All the boys think this sultry, deep-sea diva would be a great catch

Ernie & Bernie

Sykes' sidekicks, they go together like peanut butter and jellyfish

Crazy Joe

Lives alone because he's shellfish

Shortie subjects

Q: What do the shorties watch on weekends?

Saturday morning *carp*toons!

Q: Who is the shorties' favorite comic-book hero?

The caped cod!

Q: Why did the shorties cross the road?

To get to the other tide!

Q: How do the shorties get to school?

By octobus!

Q: Are the shorties anemonies?

No, they're all friends.

JUMBO TRON

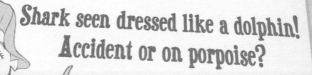

TODAYS NEWS

Seahorse ballet gets wave reviews!

*Thousands of pilgrim fish
visit holy mackerel!*

*Lino says missing seashell scandal
"A bunch abalone!"*

Off-key symphony saved by piano tuna!

*Shark seen dressed like a dolphin!
Accident or on porpoise?*

WELCOME TO THE HAMMER HOOD

Q: How do you spell fish backwards?

F-I-S-H B-A-C-K-W-A-R-D-S.

Q: How could the dolphin afford to buy a house?

He prawned everything!

Q: What kind of fish purrs?

A catfish.

Q: Where do shellfish go to borrow money?

A: To the prawn broker!

Q: Where does seaweed look for a job?

A: In the Kelp-Wanted ads!

Q: What kind of horse can swim underwater without coming up for air?

A: A seahorse!

Oscar: Knock! Knock!

Crazy Joe: Who's there?

Oscar: Crab!

Crazy Joe: Crab who?

Oscar: Crab your bathing suit. We're going for a swim!

Luca: Knock! Knock!

Lenny: Who's there?

Luca: Luca!

Lenny: Luca who?

Luca: Luca through the keyhole and see for yourself!

Oscar: Knock! Knock!

Angie: Who's there?

Oscar: Oscar!

Angie: Oscar who?

Oscar: Oscar a silly question, get a silly answer!

Lenny: Knock! Knock!

Oscar: Who's there?

Lenny: Lenny!

Oscar: Lenny who?

Lenny: Lenny in! I'm hiding from my dad!

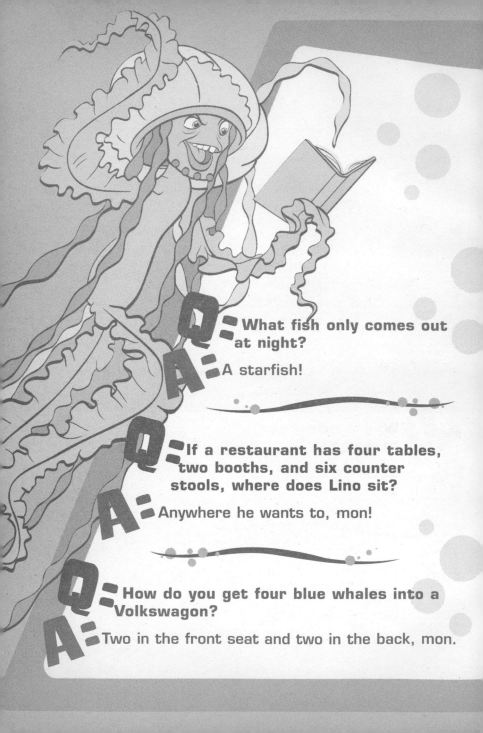

Q: What fish only comes out at night?

A: A starfish!

Q: If a restaurant has four tables, two booths, and six counter stools, where does Lino sit?

A: Anywhere he wants to, mon!

Q: How do you get four blue whales into a Volkswagon?

A: Two in the front seat and two in the back, mon.

Q: Hey mon, what do you call a fish with no eyes?

A: Fsh!

Q: What kind of noise annoys an oyster, mon?

A: Noisy noise annoys an oyster!

Q: Why is a fish easy to weigh?

A: Because it has its own scales!

Q: What is a dolphin's favorite TV show?

A: Whale of Fortune!

"Somewhere over the rainbow trout..."
"You take my air bubbles away..."
sad love songs
"Twinkle, twinkle little starfish..."

hip-hop till you flop

Q: What kind of turtle can you never trust?

A: A *turtle* tale!

Q: Where do fish wash?

A: In a river basin!

Q: What kind of fish do you call when your piano needs fixing?

A: A tuna fish.

Show me the Bling-Bling

Q: Why didn't Noah ever catch fish while he was on the ark?

A: He only brought two worms.

Q: Who was famous for robbing banks under the sea?

A: Billy the Squid!

Q: What was the Tsar of Russia's favorite fish?

A: Tsardines!

Q: Who was the greatest fish to ever play baseball?

A: Mickey Manta ray.

Lenny: Knock! Knock!

Oscar: Who's there?

Lenny: Seal.

Oscar: Seal who?

Lenny: Seal your envelope before you mail it!

DOWN WITH THAT

NO BONES ABOUT IT

Lola: Knock! Knock!

Oscar: Who's there?

Lola: Handsome.

Oscar: Handsome who?

Lola: Hand some love this way, handsome!

Angie: Knock! Knock!

Cykes: Who's there?

Angie: Calamari.

Cykes: Calamari who?

Angie: Calamari— she's looking for you.!

Bernie: Knock! Knock!

Ernie: Who's there?

Bernie: Smee.

Ernie: Smee who?

Bernie: Smee, your brother, mon!

SLAP ME SOME FIN

DOWN HERE IS ALL ABOUT REEF SMARTS

Oscar: Knock! Knock!

Crazy Joe: Who's there?

Oscar: A haddock.

Crazy Joe: A haddock who?

Oscar: Are you getting a haddock from all these knock-knock jokes?

"Her name is Lola, she is a babe fish
Guys in coral reef think she's a reel dish
She can cha-cha and do the swim
While she spends old gents' money
She winks and calls them honey
She goes out dancing, sometimes romancing

Her eyes are lovely pools
Gents love to give her jewels!
At the Coral! Coral Cabana
Deep off the coast of Louisiana
At the Coral! Coral Cabana
Lola thrills us up to our gills
At the Coral . . . We fell in love!"

Shorty: Hey, Oscar! Why are goldfish gold?

Oscar: Salt water makes them rusty.

Shorty: Hey, Oscar! Who are the dumbest fish in the ocean?

Oscar: Sardines! They lock themselves inside their can and leave the key outside.

Shorty: Hey, Oscar! How come that ship on the bottom of the ocean is always shaking?

Oscar: It's a nervous wreck.

Shorty: Hey Oscar! Who are your favorite musicians?

Oscar: Missy Halibut, Manta Ray Blige, Will Fish, and Christuna Aguilera

Ernie: Why do you always wash before committing a crime?

Bernie: Because I want to make a clean getaway, mon!

Ernie: Where do you go to clean up?

Bernie: To a river basin.

Ernie: Me, I sometimes just wash up on the shore.

Bernie: I'm thinking of starting my own business, mon.

Ernie: Really? What kind of business?

Bernie: A jellycatessen.

Ernie: I took my girlfriend to the West Indies for a vacation.

Bernie: Jamaica?

Ernie: No, mon, she wanted to go.

Bernie: I went to the hospital, but got cheated by a phony doctor!

Ernie: A phony doctor?

Bernie: Yeah, mon. He was a plastic sturgeon.

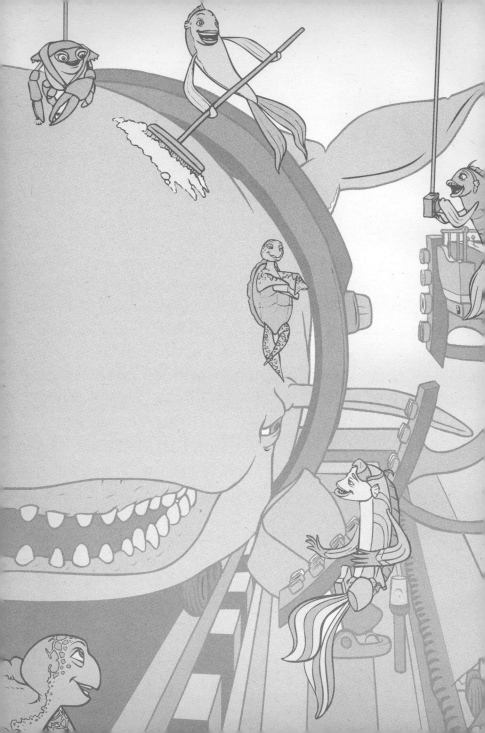

Q: What's the difference between a fisherman and one of the shorties?

A: One baits his hooks, the other hates his books!

Q: What's the difference between a fish that got caught and a fish that carefully ate the worm and got away?

A: The one that got away waited with baited breath!

Q: What's the difference between a manta ray by himself, and a manta ray by a shark's mouth?

A: The second manta will soon be an ex-ray!

Q: What's the difference between tuna and clown fish?

A: Clown fish taste funny!

Q: Hey, mon! What do whales like to chew?

A: Blubber gum!

Q: Hey, mon! Why are manatees so wrinkled?

A: Have you ever tried to iron one?

Q: Hey, mon! What do you do with a blue whale?

A: Try to cheer him up.

Q: Hey, mon! Are shellfish warm?

A: No, they're clammy!

Q: Hey, mon! What do you call a fish with two knees?

A: A two-knee fish!

SCHOOL XING

Q: Why doesn't Sykes ever have to pay cash at a restaurant?

A: He uses a credit cod!

Q: What does Sykes do in a noisy night club?

A: He uses a herring aid!

Q: Why doesn't Sykes ever go to lunch with a seagull?

A: He's afraid he'll get stuck with the bill.

Q: What newspaper does Sykes read every day?

A: The Walrus Street Journal.

Q: What part of Sykes weighs the most?

A: His scales!

Coming Soon
ROCK LOBSTER

HAMMER HEADS ARDWARE

SAVE THE WHALES! TRADE THEM FOR VALUABLE PRIZES!

TRY OUR SEA SAWS

Classified Ads

Free Tickets Available For Hit Game Show.
Whale Of Fortune.

Jobs For Seaweed -
See The Kelp Wanted Section.

Join Our Seaside Singles Club!
Object: Buoys Meet Gulls.

Executive Sea Turtle Needed -
Must Be Able To Make Snap Decisions.

"Underwater" Grades In School?
Our Tutors Will Help You Raise Them Above Sea Level!

sale!

Q: What's yellow, has four wheels and claws?

A: A taxi crab!

Q: What fish goes up the river at 100mph?

A: A motor pike!

Q: What's the best way for fish to go into business?

A: Start on a small scale!

Q: What did the boy octopus sing to the girl octopus?

A: "I wanna hold your hand, hand, hand, hand, hand, hand, hand, hand!"

Q: What's the saddest fish in the sea?

A: A blue whale!

LAST LAUGHS!

Oscar: Why are fish no good at tennis?

Angie: We don't like to get too close to the net!

Bernie: Why did the jellyfish's wife leave him?

Ernie: Too many stinging comments, mon!

Sykes: What does an octopus wear on a cold day?

Luca: A coat of arms!